THIS WALKER BOOK BELONGS TO:

SAM HALL

with love from

G-Kate

"you are a great cook!"

N|L

For Kit
V. F.

For Mark
R. B-M.

First published 1991 by
Walker Books Ltd, 87 Vauxhall Walk
London SE11 5HJ

This edition published 1995

2 4 6 8 10 9 7 5 3 1

Text © 1991 Vivian French
Illustrations © 1991 Rowan Barnes-Murphy

This book has been typeset in Sabon.

Printed in Hong Kong

British Library Cataloguing in Publication Data
A catalogue record for this book is
available from the British Library.

ISBN 0-7445-3793-2 (hb)
ISBN 0-7445-3650-2 (pb)

BAKER BEN

Written by Vivian French

Conceived and illustrated by
Rowan Barnes-Murphy

WALKER BOOKS
AND SUBSIDIARIES
LONDON • BOSTON • SYDNEY

It's very early. Ting-a-ling-a-ling!
Baker Ben's alarm clock is ringing.
"Oof!" he yawns.

Ben gets dressed and goes downstairs to his bakery.

"It's a special day today," he sings.

Ben looks on the shelves.

"Yes, everything is here!" he says.

Ben measures out flour, salt, yeast and water to make the bread.

After lighting the oven,
he mixes the ingredients
together to make a dough.

BRRRRM! goes the mixer.

Ben kneads the dough into different shapes and puts them in the oven.

He sets the clock.

Next, Ben mixes the butter, sugar, eggs, flour, sultanas and cherries together. He makes lots of little cakes and one big special cake.

He puts them into the oven.

Ting-a-ling-a-ling!

The clock is ringing.

The bread and cakes are ready now.

Ben decorates the big special cake very carefully.

"Nine o'clock!" says Ben.

"I'd better open the shop."

Doctor Elsie and Little Elsie
come in to buy some bread.
"Can I have a piece of that cake?"

asks Little Elsie.

"Not just now," says Ben.

"Come back at closing time."

Baker Ben is busy all day. Everyone says, "What a lovely cake!"

"Come back at five," says Ben, as
he wraps up bread and little cakes.

At five o'clock, Ben shuts the shop.
All his friends are there.

He lights the candles on the
big special cake.

"It's my birthday today!" Ben says
happily, and everybody cheers.

MORE WALKER PAPERBACKS
For You to Enjoy

DOCTOR ELSIE
by Vivian French / Rowan Barnes-Murphy

A delightful first "job" book about the daily routine of a busy doctor
and the implements she uses to carry out her tasks.

0-7445-3649-9   £3.99

ONE BALLERINA TWO
by Vivian French / Jan Ormerod

Two young ballerinas, one small and one not-so-small, practise
their steps and movements – from ten pliés to one final hug!

"Jan Ormerod's skill in capturing exactly the movements and gestures of
small children is shown here to great effect... A witty and informative
picture book." *The School Librarian*

0-7445-3045-8   £3.99

BUSY DAYS
by Rosalinda Kightley

Simple rhyming words and bright, bold pictures invite young children
to join two familiar workers as they go about their daily tasks.

The Postman   0-7445-3035-0
The Farmer   0-7445-3036-9
£3.99 each